SNAIL & WORM

AGAIN

Written & Illustrated
by Tina Kügler

Houghton Mifflin Harcourt
Boston   New York

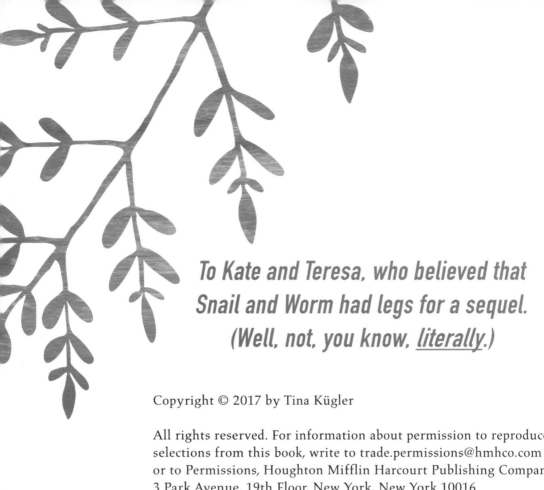

*To Kate and Teresa, who believed that
Snail and Worm had legs for a sequel.
(Well, not, you know, <u>literally</u>.)*

www.hmhco.com

The text of this book is set in Aldus LT Std.
Tina used acrylic on pastel paper, collage, and digital media to create
the illustrations. No snails or worms were harmed in the making of
this book.

Library of Congress Cataloging-in-Publication Data is on file.

ISBN 978-0-544-79249-4

Manufactured in USA
PHX 4500706135

SNAIL'S WINGS

Hey! Wow!

What is going on?

What will you do
with your wings?

Well, I don't know.
I suppose I will
fly away.

Oh.

Don't you like my wings?

Why, yes—they are lovely.
But I will be sad if you fly away.

Oh.

I did not think of that.

Hey, my wings flew
away without me!

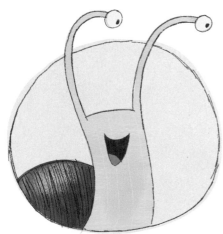

You know what?
I am glad.
I will not fly away.

I am glad too.

Boy, I was NOT ready for wings.

THE MIRROR

Hey, look!
I found something.
Come and see!

What is it?

It is a mirror.
Look at me.
Look at my reflection
in this mirror.

Are you sure that
is a mirror?

Yes, of course.
I am so handsome.

I did not know I was so handsome.

Are you *sure* that is
your reflection?

Why, yes.
Look at my
handsome chin.

But there is a beard
on that chin.
You do not have
a beard.

I don't?

Well, look at my handsome ears.

You don't have ears.

What?!

What about my
handsome wavy hair?

You don't have any
hair, either.
That is not you.

It isn't me?

Then who is it?

It is me.

I did not know I was
so handsome.

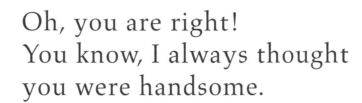

Oh, you are right!
You know, I always thought
you were handsome.

Especially your ears.

SNAIL IS SAD

Good morning!
Do you want to play?

I don't think so.

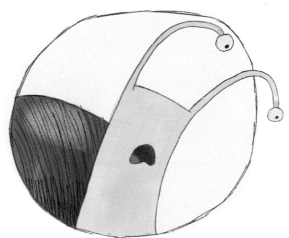

What is the matter?
You look sad.

My shell is
so plain.
I wish my shell
were special.

Look at that
beautiful beetle.
I wish my shell
looked like that.

Your shell has stripes
like the beetle's shell.

I suppose it does.

But look at these pretty rocks.
I wish my shell looked like that.

Your shell is shiny
like those rocks.

I guess it is.

But look at this
orange flower.
I wish my shell
looked like that.

Your shell is
orange, too. See?

Hmm. I never noticed that.
You are right.

Your shell is all of
those things together.
But it is also different.
It is yours.

I did not think of that.
Thank you.
You are a good friend.

I almost feel better now.

Almost?

I really wish I could ride a bicycle.